MR. STRONG

by Roger Hargreaves

WORLD INTERNATIONAL

This is the story of Mr Strong.

Mr Strong is the strongest person in the whole wide world.

The strongest person there ever has been, and probably the strongest person there ever will be.

He is so strong he can not only bend an iron bar with his bare hands, he can tie knots in it!

Mr Strong is so strong he can throw a cannonball as far as you or I can throw a tennis ball!

Mr Strong is so strong he can hammer nails into a wall just by tapping them with his finger.

Strong by name and strong by nature!

And would you like to know the secret of Mr Strong's strength?

Eggs!

The more eggs Mr Strong eats, the stronger he becomes.

Stronger and stronger and stronger!

Anyway, this story is about a funny thing that happened to Mr Strong one day.

That morning he was having breakfast.

And for breakfast he was having . . .eggs!

Followed by eggs. And to finish, he was having –
guess what?

That's right. Eggs!

That was Mr Strong's normal breakfast.

After his eggy breakfast Mr Strong cleaned his teeth.

And, as usual, he squeezed all the toothpaste out of the tube.

And, as usual, he cleaned his teeth so hard he broke his toothbrush.

Mr Strong gets through a lot of toothpaste and toothbrushes!

After that he decided to take a walk.

He put on his hat and opened the front door of his house. Crash!

"What a beautiful day," he thought to himself and, stepping outside his house, he shut his front door.

Bang! The door fell off its hinges.

Mr Strong gets through a lot of front doors!

Then Mr Strong went for his walk.

He walked through the woods.

But, he wasn't looking where he was going, and walked slap bang into a huge tree. Crack!

The huge tree trunk snapped and the tree thundered to the ground.

"Whoops!" said Mr Strong.

He walked into town.

And again, not looking where he was going, he walked slap bang straight into a bus.

Now, as you know, if you or I were to walk into a bus, we'd get run over.

Wouldn't we?

Not Mr Strong!

The bus stopped as if it had run into a brick wall.

"Whoops!" said Mr Strong.

Eventually Mr Strong walked through the town and out into the country. To a farm.

The farmer met him in the road looking very worried.

"What's the matter?" asked Mr Strong.

"It's my cornfield," replied the farmer. "It's on fire and I can't put it out!"

Mr Strong looked over the hedge, and sure enough the cornfield was blazing fiercely.

"Water," said Mr Strong. "We must get water to put out the fire!"

"But I don't have enough water to put a whole field out," cried the worried farmer, "and the nearest water is down at the river, and I don't have a pump!"

"Then we'll have to find something to carry the water," replied Mr Strong.

"Is that your barn?" he asked the farmer, pointing to a barn in another field.

"Yes, I was going to put my corn in it," said the farmer. "But . . ."

"Can I use it?" asked Mr Strong.

"Yes, but . . .," replied the perplexed farmer.

Mr Strong walked over to the barn, and then do you know what he did?

He picked it up. He actually picked up the barn!

The farmer couldn't believe his eyes.

Then Mr Strong carried the barn, above his head, down to the river.

Then he turned the barn upside down.

Then he lowered it into the river so that it filled up with water.

Then, and this shows how strong Mr Strong is, he picked it up and carried it back to the blazing cornfield.

Mr Strong emptied the upside down barn full of water over the flames.

Sizzle. Sizzle. Splutter. Splutter.

One minute the flames were leaping into the air. The next minute they'd gone.

"However can I thank you?" the farmer asked Mr Strong.

"Oh, it was nothing," remarked Mr Strong modestly.

"But I must find some way to reward you," said the farmer.

"Well," said Mr Strong, "you're a farmer, so you must keep chickens."

"Yes, lots," said the farmer.

"And chickens lay eggs," went on Mr Strong, "and I rather like eggs!"

"Then you shall have as many eggs as you can carry," said the farmer, and took Mr Strong over to the farmyard.

Mr Strong said goodbye to the farmer, and thanked him for the eggs, and the farmer thanked him for helping.

Then Mr Strong, just using one finger, picked up the eggs and went home.

Mr Strong put the eggs carefully down on his kitchen table and went to close the kitchen door.

Crash! The door fell off its hinges.

"Whoops!" said Mr Strong, and sat down.

Crunch! The chair fell to bits.

"Whoops!" said Mr Strong, and started cooking his lunch. And for lunch he was starting with eggs. Followed by an egg or two. And then eggs. And then for his pudding he was having . . .

Well, can you guess? If you can, there's no need to turn this page over to find out that he was having . . .

Ice cream!

Ha! Ha!

MORE SPECIAL OFFERS
FOR MR MEN AND LITTLE MISS READERS

In every Mr Men and Little Miss book like this one, and now in the Mr Men sticker and activity books, you will find a special token. Collect six tokens and we will send you a gift of your choice.

Choose either a Mr Men or Little Miss poster, or a Mr Men or Little Miss **double sided** full colour bedroom door hanger.

Return this page with six tokens per gift required to Marketing Dept., MM / LM Gifts, World International Ltd., Deanway Technology Centre, Wilmslow Road, Handforth, Cheshire SK9 3FB

|— 100 mm —|

Your name:_____ Age: _____

Address: _____

_____

_____Postcode: _____

Parent / Guardian Name (Please Print) _____

Please tape a 20p coin to your request to cover part post and package cost

I enclose six tokens per gift, please send me:-

Posters:-	Mr Men Poster ☐	Little Miss Poster ☐
Door Hangers -	Mr Nosey / Muddle ☐	Mr Greedy / Lazy ☐
	Mr Tickle / Grumpy ☐	Mr Slow / Quiet ☐
	Mr Messy / Noisy ☐	
	L Miss Fun / Late ☐	L Miss Helpful / Tidy ☐
	L Miss Busy / Brainy ☐	L Miss Star / Fun ☐

Please Tick Appropriate Box

We may occasionally wish to advise you of other Mr Men gifts. If you would rather we didn't please tick this box ☐

ENTRANCE FEE SAUSAGES

MR.GREEDY

250 mm

Collect six of these tokens
You will find one inside every
Mr Men and Little Miss book
which has this special offer.

1
TOKEN

Offer open to residents of UK, Channel Isles and Ireland only

Mr Men and Little Miss Library Presentation Boxes

In response to the many thousands of requests for the above, we are delighted to advise that these are now available direct from ourselves,
for only £4.99 (inc VAT) plus 50p p & p.
The full colour units accommodate each complete library. They have an integral carrying handle and "push out" bookmark as well as a neat stay closed fastener.
Please do not send cash in the post. Cheques should be made payable to **World International Ltd. for the sum of £5.49** (inc p & p) per box.
Return this page with your cheque, stating below which presentation box you would like,
**to Mr Men Office, World International Ltd.,
Deanway Technology Centre, Wilmslow Road, Handforth, Cheshire SK9 3FB.**

Your Name _____

Your Address _____

_____

_____ Post Code _____

Name of Parent/Guardian (please print) _____

Signature _____

I enclose a cheque for £ _____ made payable to World International Ltd.

Please send me a Mr Men Presentation Box ☐ (please tick or write in quantity)

Little Miss Presentation Box ☐

Offer applies to UK, Eire & Channel Isles only.

Thank you